a minedition book
published by Penguin Young Readers Group

Published simultaneously in Canada.
Manufactured in Hong Kong by Wide World Ltd.
Designed by Michael Neugebauer
Typesetting in Veljovic, designed by Jovica Veljovic.
Color separation by Fotoreproduzioni Grafiche, Verona, Italy.

Library of Congress Cataloging-in-Publication Data available upon request.

ISBN 978-0-698-40001-6
10 9 8 7 6 5 4 3

For more information please visit our website: www.minedition.com

The Little Mermaid

Hans Christian Andersen
with Pictures by Lisbeth Zwerger

Translated from the Danish by
Anthea Bell

Jubilee Edition
200 years Hans Christian Andersen
50 years Lisbeth Zwerger

$\mathcal{F}$ar away out at sea, the water is as blue as the petals of the most beautiful cornflower and as clear as the purest glass, but it is very deep, deeper than any anchor chain will reach. You would have to stand many church towers on top of each other before one came up above the water from the bottom of the sea. And down there the merfolk live.

You mustn't think, however, that there's nothing but white sand at the bottom of the sea — no, the strangest trees and plants grow there, with stems and leaves so supple that they move at the slightest touch of the water as if they were alive. Fish large and small swim among their branches, just as birds fly through the trees up here in the air. The sea king's castle lies in the deepest place of all. Its walls are made of coral and its tall, pointed windows of the clearest amber, but the roof is made of seashells that open and close as the water flows by. They are very beautiful, for each shell contains a shining pearl, and any one of them is a jewel fit for a queen's crown.

The sea king had been a widower for many years, and his old mother kept house for him. She was a clever woman, but proud of her noble birth, so she wore twelve oysters on her tail. Other noble mermen and mermaids were only allowed six. In every other way she was an excellent woman, particularly because she loved the little sea princesses her granddaughters so much. There were six of them, and they were all pretty children, but the youngest was the loveliest of all. Her skin was as clear and delicate as a rose petal, her eyes as blue as the deepest sea, but like all the other merfolk she had no feet, and her body ended in a fishtail.

The princesses could play down in the castle all day long, in the great halls where living flowers grew out of the walls. When the great amber windows were opened the fish swam through them, just as swallows fly through our own windows when we open them, and the fish swam straight to the little princesses, ate from their hands, and let the girls stroke them.

There was a large garden outside the castle, with trees of fiery red and dark blue. The fruit of those trees shone like gold, and their blossoms were like bright flames, always moving the stems and leaves. The ground where they grew was the finest sand, but it was the hue of a blue flame, and indeed a strange, shimmering blue light surrounded everything down there; you might have thought you were high up in the air, with nothing but the sky above and below, instead of down on the bed of the sea. When there was no wind you could see the sun, like a crimson flower with light streaming from its cupped petals.

Each of the little princesses had her own small garden plot where she could dig and plant just as she liked.

One of the mermaid princesses gave her garden the shape of a whale, another shaped hers like a little mermaid, but the youngest made hers as round as the sun, and planted flowers that shone red like the sun too. She was a strange child, quiet and dreamy, and when the other sisters decorated their gardens with the wonderful things they had taken from shipwrecks she wanted nothing but the rose-red flowers that looked like the sun in the sky above, and a pretty marble statue. It was a statue of a beautiful boy carved in clear white stone, and it had been washed down from a wrecked ship to the bottom of the sea. She planted a rose-red weeping willow by the statue; the tree grew and flourished, and its fresh branches hung down to the blue sandy ground where the shadows were violet and kept moving with the movement of the tree. It looked as if the ends of the branches and the tree roots wanted to kiss.

The little mermaid's greatest pleasure was to hear tales of the human world above. She made her old grandmother tell all the stories she knew about ships and cities, men and women and animals. The most wonderful thing of all, she thought, was that flowers were scented in the world above, for they had no fragrance at all at the bottom of the sea, and the woods up there were green, and the fish flying among the trees sang so loud and beautifully that it was a joy to hear them.

Those fish, of course, were really little birds, but the girls' grandmother called them fish because otherwise the mermaids, who had never yet seen a bird, wouldn't have understood.

"When you are fifteen years old," said their grandmother, "you will be allowed to come up out of the sea, sit on the rocks in the moonlight, and watch the big ships sailing by. And then you will see forests and cities!"

Next year one of the sisters would be fifteen, but as for the others, each was a year younger than the sister before her, so it would be a whole five years before the youngest of them could come up from the bottom of the sea and find out what our world looks like. But each sister promised the others to tell them what she had seen and what she thought most beautiful on that first day, because their grandmother hadn't told them nearly enough, and there was so much that they wanted to know.

None of them wanted to see the world above as much as the youngest — and she was the very one who had the longest to wait and was so quiet and dreamy. On many a night she stood by the open window looking up through the dark blue water where the fish swam, moving their fins and tails. She could see the moon and the stars, pale as they were, but through the water they looked much larger than they do to our eyes. And if something like a black cloud moved among them she knew it was either a whale swimming over her or a ship full of human beings, who had no idea that a pretty little mermaid was standing down below, stretching her white hands up to the ship's keel.

Then the eldest princess's fifteenth birthday came, and she was allowed to go up above the surface of the sea.

When she came back she had a hundred tales to tell, but the best thing of all, she said, had been to lie on a sandbank by moonlight in the calm sea, looking at the great city on the coast nearby. The lights in that city sparkled like a hundred stars, you could hear music and all the sounds of carriages and men and women, and you could see the church towers and listen to the bells ringing. It was because she couldn't go there that she longed for it most of all.

Oh, how eagerly the youngest sister listened, and later, when she stood by the open window in the evening and looked up through the dark blue water, she thought of the great city with all its sound and noise, and then it seemed to her that she could hear the church bells ringing all the way down to her there in the sea.

Next year the second sister was allowed to come up out of the water and swim wherever she wanted. She came up above the surface just as the sun was setting, and she thought the sunset the most beautiful thing she had ever seen. The whole sky had looked like gold, she said, and as for the clouds, she couldn't begin to describe their beauty! They had sailed away over her, red and violet, but a flock of wild swans like a long white veil flew over the water toward the sun, moving even faster than the clouds. She swam toward the sun herself, but then it sank, and the rosy glow faded from the surface of the sea and from the clouds.

The year after that it was the third sister's turn. She was very daring, so she swam up a broad river that flowed into the sea. She saw beautiful green hills where vineyards grew, and castles and citadels looked out from magnificent forests; she heard all the birds singing, and the sun shining down was so hot that she often had to dive under the water to cool her burning face. In a little bay she met a whole crowd of small human children, running around naked and splashing in the water.

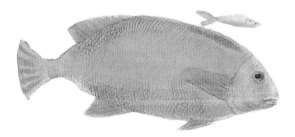

She wanted to play with them, but they ran away in fright, and along came a little black animal. It was a dog, but she had never seen a dog before, and it barked at her so alarmingly that she took fright and swam back into the open sea, but she could never forget the wonderful forests, the green hills, and the sweet little children who could swim in the water even though they had no fishtails.

The fourth sister was not so bold, and she stayed out in the middle of the wild waves and told her sisters that it was best of all there. You could see for many miles around, and the sky was like a great glass bell above the sea. She had seen ships, but only at a great distance. They looked like seagulls, and there had been playful dolphins turning somersaults, while great whales blew jets of water from their nostrils, as if hundreds of fountains were playing.

Next it was the fifth sister's turn. Her birthday happened to be in winter, so she saw something that the others hadn't seen at all the first time they went above the waves. The sea was green, and there were great icebergs floating on it looking like pearls, she said, much taller than the church towers built by human beings. The icebergs were all kinds of wonderful shapes and glittered as brightly as diamonds. She had climbed on one of the biggest, and all the sailing ships cruised around her in fear as she sat there letting her long hair blow in the wind. But as evening came on the sky was overcast with clouds and there was thunder and lightning, while the black sea lifted up great blocks of ice that shone as the lightning flashed. The sails on all the ships were hauled in, and there was fear and terror aboard. The fifth mermaid sat calmly on her floating iceberg, watching blue lightning zigzag down into the shining sea.

Whenever one of the sisters first came up above the water she was enchanted by all the new and beautiful things she saw, but now that the older mermaids were grown girls and could come up whenever they liked, they soon lost interest. They wanted to go home again, and by the end of a month they were saying it was best to be back at the bottom of the sea where everything was so pretty.

In the evenings the five sisters often linked arms and came up to the surface of the sea in a long line. They had beautiful voices, lovelier than any human voice, and when a storm was coming up and they could tell that ships would capsize, they swam ahead of the vessels singing wonderful songs of the beautiful sights to be seen on the sea bed, and telling the sailors not to be afraid of going down there. But the sailors could not understand the words. They thought that all they heard was the sound of the storm, and they never saw the wonderful things down in the sea either, because when a ship sank its crew drowned, and they were dead by the time they reached the sea king's castle.

When her elder sisters rose through the water in the evening arm in arm, their little sister stood all alone watching them go, and she felt she would weep, but mermaids cannot shed tears, so she suffered all the more.

"Oh, if only I were fifteen!" she said. "I know I shall love the world up above and the people who live there!"

At last her fifteenth birthday came.

"There, now you're off our hands," said her grandmother the old dowager queen. "Come along, let me dress you up as I did your sisters!" And she put a wreath of white lilies in her hair. Each flower petal was half a pearl, and the old lady found eight large oysters to clasp the princess's tail as a sign of her high rank.

"Oh, it hurts!" said the little mermaid.

"One must suffer for the sake of beauty!" said the old lady.

The little mermaid would have liked to be rid of all this finery, and wanted to take the heavy wreath out of her hair; the red flowers in her garden looked much prettier, but there was nothing she could do about it. "Goodbye," she said, and she rose up through the water as light and clear as a bubble.

The sun had just set when she raised her head above the surface, but all the clouds were still glowing like roses and gold, and in the middle of the pale pink sky the evening star shone bright and beautiful. The air was fresh and mild, and the sea was very calm. There lay a great ship with three masts. Only one sail was hoisted, for there was no wind at all, and the sailors were sitting all around in the rigging and on the yardarm.

There was music and singing, and as the evening twilight fell hundreds of lights of every hue were lit. They looked as if the flags of all nations were flying. The little mermaid swam right up to the porthole of a cabin, and whenever the water lifted her she could look through the glass, which shone like a mirror, and see a great many finely dressed people inside. The most handsome of them all was a young prince who had big black eyes and couldn't have been more than sixteen years old. In fact it was his birthday, and that was the reason for all this magnificence. The sailors danced on deck, and when the young prince stepped out on the deck himself more than a hundred rockets shot into the air. They shone as bright as day, so that the little mermaid was frightened and went down under the water, but she soon put her head above the surface again, and thought it looked as if all the stars were falling out of the sky. She had never seen such fireworks before. Huge wheels like suns let off sparks, magnificent fiery fish shapes flew through the blue air, and it was all reflected in the clear, still sea. The ship itself was so brightly lit that you could see every cable in the rigging. And oh, how handsome the young prince was, shaking hands with everyone and smiling while the music echoed through the air of the fine night.

It grew late, but the little mermaid couldn't take her eyes off the ship and the handsome prince. The bright lights went out, no more rockets rose in the air, and the cannon stopped firing, but deep down in the sea there was a rumbling and a growling noise. She stayed there in the water, rocking up and down so that she could see into the cabin. But now the ship began to move faster, sail after sail was hoisted and the waves were rising, huge clouds came up and lightning flashed in the distance. There was going to be a terrible storm, so the sailors reefed in the sails.

The great ship tossed as it raced over the rough sea. The water rose like tall black mountains about to crash down on the mainmast, but the ship went down between the great waves and rode up again on the towering water like a swan. It looked great fun to the little mermaid, but it was no fun at all for the sailors; the ship creaked and groaned, the thick planks gave way under the buffeting of the waves, the sea came rushing into the ship, the mainmast snapped like a reed and the vessel tipped over on its side, with water flowing in. Now the little mermaid saw that they were in danger; even she had to be careful to avoid the drifting planks and other flotsam from the ship. For a moment everything was so dark that she could see nothing at all, but when the lightning flashed it was bright again, and she could see all the people on board; stumbling about and trying to keep on their feet as best they could. She looked around for the young prince in particular, and just as the ship split in two she saw him fall into the deep sea. She was glad, because now he would go down to her. But then she remembered that human beings cannot live in water, and he would be dead by the time he reached her father's castle. No, no, he mustn't die! She swam among the beams and planks floating on the sea, and quite forgot that they could crush her. She went down deep below the water and came up through the waves again, and so at last she reached the young prince, who could hardly swim any longer in the stormy sea. His arms and legs were beginning to tire, and his beautiful eyes were closing. He would certainly have drowned if the little mermaid had not reached him. But she held his head above the water and let the waves drive her with him wherever they wanted.

In the morning the storm was over, but there was no sign of the ship. The sun rose from the sea as red and bright as if it brought life back to the prince's cheeks, but his eyes were still closed. The mermaid kissed his high, beautiful brow and stroked back his wet hair. She thought he looked like the marble statue in her little garden; she kissed him again and willed him to live.

Now she saw land ahead, tall blue mountains with the white snow shining on their peaks as if swans had settled there. Down on the coast there were beautiful green forests, and in the woods there was a church or a monastery, she was not sure which, but it was a building. Lemon and orange trees grew in its garden, and there were tall palm trees at the gateway. The water was calm but very deep here, with the sea forming a little bay that went right up to the rocks and the fine white sand that had been washed up around them. She swam to the rocks with the handsome prince and laid him down on the sand, making sure that his head was raised and lay in the warm sunshine.

Then bells rang inside the large white building, and a great many young girls came walking through the garden. The little mermaid swam out again behind some tall rocks rising above the water, covered her hair and breast with sea foam so that no one could see her little face, and waited to see who would find the poor prince.

Before long a young girl saw him. She seemed greatly alarmed, but only for a moment. Then she fetched many other people, and the mermaid saw the prince revive and smile at everyone around him. But he never looked out to sea to smile at her; after all, he didn't know that she had saved him. She felt so sad that when he was taken away into the big building she plunged sadly down into the water and returned to her father's castle.

She had always been a quiet, thoughtful girl, but she was even quieter now. Her sisters asked what she had seen up above the water, but she did not tell them.

On many a morning and evening she came up from the sea at the place where she had left the prince. She saw the fruits in the garden ripening and being picked; she saw the snow melting on the high mountains. But she never saw the prince, so she always went home even sadder than before. Her one comfort was to sit in her little garden and put her arms around the pretty marble statue that looked like the prince, but she neglected her flowers. They grew wild all over the paths and twined their long stems and their leaves into the branches of the trees, so that it was quite dark in her garden.

In the end she could bear it no longer, and told one of her sisters her story. All the other sisters immediately heard it too, but no one else knew except for a few other mermaids who told no one at all except their very closest friends. And one of those friends knew who the prince was; she herself had seen the birthday party on board the ship, and she knew where he came from and where his kingdom lay.

"Come along, little sister!" said the other princesses, and with their arms around each other they rose from the sea in a long line just where they knew the prince's castle stood.

It was built of shining, pale yellow stone, with great flights of marble steps. One of these stairways went straight down to the sea. Magnificent gilded domes rose above the roof, and among the columns that surrounded the whole building stood statues that might have been alive. You could look through the clear glass of the tall windows and see into the most magnificent halls, where costly silk drapery and tapestries hung, and there were great paintings all over the walls. It was a pleasure to look at them. In the middle of the largest hall a great fountain played. Its jets of water rose high to the ceiling and the glass dome above, through which sunlight shone down on the water and the beautiful plants growing in the wide basin of the fountain.

Now the little mermaid knew where the prince lived, and she swam to the castle again on many evenings and nights. She came much closer to land than any of the other mermaids had dared, she even went right up the narrow channel beneath the handsome marble balcony that cast its long shadow over the water. She would sit there gazing at the young prince when he thought he was all alone in the bright moonlight.

On many evenings she saw him sailing out in his fine boat, with flags flying and music playing. She peeped through the green reeds, and when the wind caught her long, silvery white veil and people saw it, they thought it was a swan spreading its wings.

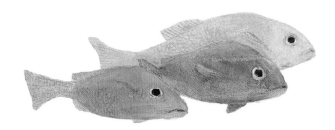

And on many a night when the fishermen put out to sea by torchlight she heard them praising the young prince, and she was glad she had saved his life when he was drifting half dead in the waves. Then she remembered how his head rested against her breast, and how lovingly she had kissed him, although he knew nothing about it, and couldn't even dream of her.

She became fonder and fonder of human beings, she longed more and more to be able to come up out of the water and mingle with them, for their world seemed to her much larger than her own. They could sail the sea in ships, they could climb the mountains that rose high above the clouds, and the lands belonging to mankind, with all their woods and fields, reached farther than her eye could see. There was so much she wanted to know, but her sisters couldn't answer her questions, so she asked her old grandmother, who knew the world of humans very well, and rightly called it the Land Above The Sea.

"If human beings don't happen to drown," asked the little mermaid, "can they live for ever? Don't they die as we do here under the sea?"

"Yes," said her old grandmother, "they must die too, and indeed their lives are even shorter than ours. We can live to three hundred years old, but when our lives here come to an end we are turned into foam on the sea, and we don't even have a place down here to be buried among our loved ones. We have no immortal souls, we never come to life again. We are like the green reeds; when they are cut down they never grow green again! Human beings, however, have souls that live for ever when the body has fallen to dust; the soul rises through the clear air and up to the shining stars! Just as we can come up above the waves and see the lands of men, so they can reach wonderful places unknown to us that we will never see."

"Why don't we have immortal souls?" asked the little mermaid sadly. "I'd give all the hundreds of years of my life to be human for a single day, and then be part of the kingdom of heaven."

"You mustn't think about such things!" said the old lady. "We are far happier and much better off than the human beings up above!"

"So I shall die and drift away like foam on the sea, and never hear the music of the waves or see the lovely flowers and the red sun any more? Is there nothing I can do to win an immortal soul?"

"No!" said the old lady. "Not unless a man were to love you so much that you meant more to him than his mother and father, unless his mind and heart were set on you, and he let the priest place his right hand in yours and vowed to keep faith with you in this world and for all eternity. Then his soul would flow into your body, and you too would have a share in human bliss. He would give you a soul, yet he would keep his own. But that can never happen! Up on earth they think your fishtail is ugly, beautiful as it is down here in the sea. They know no better; to be thought beautiful up there you have to have the two clumsy props they call legs!"

The little mermaid sighed, and looked sadly at her fishtail.

"So let us be happy," said the old lady, "let us dance and leap for joy all through the three hundred years of our lives; that's a good length of time, and then when you die you can rest content. And there's going to be a court ball this evening."

It was a more magnificent ball than any ever seen on earth. The walls and ceiling of the great ballroom were made of glass, thick but clear. Several hundred huge seashells, rosy red and grass-green, stood lined up on all sides of the room, holding blue fire that lit the whole room and shone through the walls so that the sea outside glowed with light too. You could see all the countless fish, large and small, swimming up to the glass walls; some of them had bright crimson scales, while others shone like gold or silver. A wide torrent of water flowed through the middle of the hall, and the mermen and mermaids danced on it to the sound of their own sweet singing. Earthly men and women never have such sweet voices. The little mermaid sang most beautifully of all, and they all applauded her. For a moment she felt joyful, for she knew she had a lovelier voice than anyone on earth or in the sea. But soon she began thinking of the world above again; she could not forget the handsome prince or her sorrow that she had no immortal soul. So she stole out of her father's castle while all was song and merriment inside, and sat sadly in her little garden. Then she heard the sound of a horn echo down through the water, and she thought: "He must be sailing up above there, the man I love more than father or mother, the man on whom my heart is set and in whose hands I would gladly lay my happiness. I will venture anything to win him and an immortal soul! While my sisters are still dancing there in my father's castle I'll go to visit the sea witch. I've always been afraid of her, but perhaps she can give me help and advice!"

So the little mermaid left her garden and went out into the turbulent whirlpools beyond which the witch lived. She had never gone that way before. No flowers grew there, no seagrass, there was only the bare, grey, sandy sea floor where the turbulent water went around and around like millwheels, sweeping everything that came within its grasp down to the depths with it.

She must pass through the middle of the whirlpools that crushed everything they touched to reach the domain of the sea witch, and for a long time there was no way except over the hot, gurgling mud that the witch called her moor. Beyond the mud was her house, in the middle of a strange wood. All the trees and bushes were polyps, half animal and half plant; they looked like hundred-headed snakes growing out of the ground. All their branches were long, slimy arms, with finger like supple worms, and every limb kept writhing from root to tip. They coiled around everything in the sea that they could grasp and never let it go again. The little mermaid stood there terrified, with her heart thudding, and she almost turned back, but then she thought of the prince and of a human soul, and she plucked up her courage. She bound her long, flowing hair tightly around her head, so that the polyps could not get hold of it, she clasped both hands over her breast, and so, like a fish darting through the water, she shot past the ugly polyps stretching their flexible arms and fingers out behind her. She could see that whenever one of them caught anything, its catch was held fast with hundreds of little arms like strong iron bands. The white skeletons of human beings who had perished at sea and sunk to the bottom peered out from the arms of the polyps. They clasped ship's rudders and sea chests, the skeletons of land animals, and a mermaid whom they had caught and choked to death; that was almost the worst sight of all.

Then she came to a large, marshy place in the wood where big, fat sea serpents coiled, showing their ugly, yellowish-white bellies. In the middle of this place stood a house built from the white bones of shipwrecked mariners. There sat the sea witch letting a toad eat out of her mouth, just as human beings might feed sugar to a little canary. She called the fat, ugly sea serpents her little chickens, and let them twist and turn on her broad, flabby breast.

"I know what you want," the sea witch told the mermaid. "It's a stupid wish, but you shall have it, for it will bring you bad luck, my pretty princess. You want to be rid of your fishtail and walk on two props instead, like human beings, so that the young prince will fall in love with you, and you can get both him and an immortal soul!" So saying, the witch laughed a loud, terrible laugh, making the toad and the serpents fall to the ground and writhe about there. "You've come at just the right time," she said. "Once the sun rises tomorrow it would be another year before I could help you. Well, I'll make you a potion. You must swim to land with it before sunrise, sit on the shore and drink it, and then your tail will fall off and shrink, turning into what humans call pretty legs, but it will hurt, the pain will be like a sharp sword piercing you. All who set eyes on you will think you the prettiest child they ever saw. You'll keep your grace of movement, no dancer will move as lightly as you, but every step you take will be as if you were treading on knives so sharp that you'll feel your blood is about to flow. Will you suffer all this? If so, I will help you."

"Yes!" said the little mermaid. Her voice trembled, but she thought of the prince and an immortal soul.

"Remember," said the witch, "that once you have taken human form you can never be a mermaid again! You can never go down through the water to your sisters and your father's castle any more. And if you don't win the love of the prince, making him forget mother and father, so that he sets his heart on your alone and tells the priest to join your hands in marriage, then you will not get an immortal soul! On the morning after he marries another your heart will break, and you will be foam on the sea."

"I agree," said the little mermaid, turning deathly pale.

"But you must pay me too," said the witch, "and it is no small price I ask. You have a sweeter voice than anyone here on the sea bed; you probably think you can enchant the prince with it, but you must give me your voice. I want the very best thing you have in payment for my precious potion! I have to mingle my own blood with the potion to make it as sharp as a two-edged sword!"

"But if you take my voice," said the little mermaid, "what will I have left?"

"Your pretty figure," said the witch, "your grace of movement, and your speaking eyes; you can captivate a human heart with those. Well, have you lost your courage? Put out your tongue for me to cut off as my payment, and then you can have my strong potion."

"Very well," said the little mermaid, and the witch put her cauldron on to boil the magic potion. "Cleanliness is a great virtue," she said, scouring out the cauldron with her serpents tied into a knot; and then she cut her own breast and let the black blood drip in. The steam formed strange and terrifying shapes. Every moment the witch cast something else into the cauldron, and when it was bubbling it sounded like a crocodile weeping. At last the potion was ready, and looked like the clearest water!

"There you are," said the witch, and she cut out the little mermaid's tongue, so now she was mute and could neither speak nor sing.

"If the polyps should catch you as you go back through my wood," said the witch, "sprinkle a single drop of this potion on them and their arms and fingers will break into a thousand pieces." But there was no need for the little mermaid to do that, for the polyps shrank from her in terror when they saw the bright potion shining in her hand like a twinkling star. She quickly made her way through the wood, across the moor, and through the turbulent whirlpools.

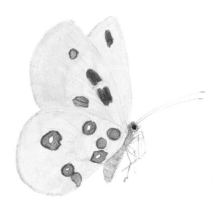

Now she could see her father's castle. The lights were out in the great ball-room, everyone inside must be asleep, but she dared not go in to see them now that she was mute and must leave them for ever. She felt as if her heart would break with grief. She stole into the garden, took a flower from each of her sisters' flowerbeds, blew thousands of kisses to the castle and then rose up through the dark blue sea.

The sun had not yet risen when she saw the prince's castle and made her way to the magnificent flight of marble steps. The moon was shining brightly. The little mermaid drank the sharp, burning potion, and it felt as if a two-edged sword were piercing her delicate body; she fainted away and lay there like the dead. When the sun rose above the sea she came back to her senses and felt a keen pain. But the handsome young prince was standing before her; when he turned his coal-black eyes on her she cast her own eyes down, and saw that her fishtail was gone and she had the sweetest little white legs on which a girl ever walked. But she was entirely naked, so she wrapped her long, luxuriant hair around herself. The prince asked who she was and how she had come there, and she looked at him gently yet very sadly with her dark blue eyes, for she could not speak. Then he took her hand and led her into the castle. Every step she took felt as if she were treading on pointed needles and sharp knives, just as the witch had warned her, but she bore it gladly. She was light as a bubble when she walked, holding the prince's hand, and he and everyone else marvelled at her beautiful, graceful movement.

She was given costly clothes of silk and muslin, and she was the fairest of all in the castle, but she was mute and could neither speak nor sing. Beautiful slave girls clad in silk and gold appeared and sang for the prince and his royal parents. One sang more sweetly than all the rest, and the prince clapped his hands and smiled at her. Then the little mermaid was sad, knowing that she herself had once sung much more sweetly, and she thought: "Oh, if he only knew that I have given up my voice for all eternity to be near him!"

Then the slave girls danced gracefully, swaying in time to the beautiful music. The little mermaid raised her lovely white arms, stood on tiptoe and hovered over the floor, dancing as no one had ever danced before; she seemed more beautiful with every movement, and her eyes spoke more deeply to the heart than all the slave girls' singing.

Everyone was enchanted by her, especially the prince, who called her his little foundling, and she danced again and again, although every time her foot touched the ground it was like treading on sharp knives. The prince said she must stay with him always, and she was allowed to sleep on a velvet cushion outside his door.

He had a man's riding habit made for her so that she could go out with him on horseback. They rode through the fragrant woods where green branches brushed their shoulders and little birds sang among the fresh leaves. She climbed high mountains with the prince, and although her tender feet bled so much that other people could see it she just laughed, and followed him until she saw the clouds sailing by below like a flock of birds flying away to foreign lands.

Back in the prince's castle, when the others were asleep at night, she would go out to the broad flight of marble steps. The cold sea water cooled her burning feet, and then she thought of the merfolk down beneath the waves.

One night her sisters came up arm in arm, singing very sadly as they swam through the water. She waved to them, and they recognized her and told her how sorrowful she had made them all. After that they visited her every night, and once, far out at sea, she saw her old grandmother, who had not been above the surface for many years, and the sea king with his crown on his head; they stretched their hands out to her, but they dared not come as close to land as her sisters.

Day by day she became dearer to the prince; he loved her as you love a good, sweet child, but it never entered his head to make her his queen, and she must be his wife or she would never have an immortal soul, but would turn to foam on the sea on his wedding morning.

"Don't you love me best of all?" the little mermaid's eyes seemed to ask when he took her in his arms and kissed her lovely forehead.

"Yes, you are dearer to me than anyone," said the prince, "for you have the best heart of all. You are so devoted to me! You are like a young girl I once saw but shall never find again. I was on a ship which was wrecked, and the waves cast me up on land near a sacred temple served by several girls. The youngest of them found me on shore and saved my life, but I saw her only twice. She is the only girl in the world I could ever love, but you are so like her that you almost drive her out of my mind; she belongs to the sacred temple, and so good fortune has sent you to me. We will never part!"

"Ah, he doesn't know that it was I who saved his life!" thought the little mermaid. "I carried him over the sea to the forest where the temple stands; I hid in the foam and waited to see if anyone would come. And I saw the beautiful girl whom he loves more than me!"

Then the mermaid sighed deeply, for she could not weep. "The girl belongs to the sacred temple, he said. She will never return to the world, they will never meet again, but I am with him, I see him every day, I will care for him, love him, give him my life!"

But now the time came when the prince, so they said, was to be married to the lovely daughter of the king who ruled the country next to his, so he was fitting out a magnificent ship. The prince is off to see that foreign land, folk told each other, but it's really the king's daughter he is going to visit, with a great retinue of companions. However, the little mermaid shook her head and smiled; she knew the prince's mind better than anyone. "I must go on my travels," he had told her, "I must see this fair princess, my parents insist on it, but they will never force me to bring her home as my bride. I cannot love her! She is not like the beautiful girl in the temple, but you are. If I were ever to choose a bride it would be you, my mute foundling with the speaking eyes!" And he kissed her red mouth, played with her long hair, and laid his head on her heart, so that she dreamed of human happiness and an immortal soul.

"You are not afraid of the sea, are you, my mute child?" he asked as they stood on the fine ship which was to carry him to the country of the king who ruled the land nearby. He told her about storms and calms, of strange fish in the deep and of sights seen by divers, and she smiled to hear his tales, for she knew better than anyone what it was really like on the bottom of the sea.

In the bright moonlit night, when everyone else was asleep except for the steersman at the wheel, she sat by the ship's rail and looked down through the clear water. She thought she saw her father's castle, and her old grandmother standing on top of it with her silver crown on her head, looking up at the ship's keel through the fast-moving water. Then her sisters came up above the water, looked sorrowfully at her and wrung their white hands. She waved to them, smiled, and wished she could tell them how happy she was, but then the ship's cabin boy came along and her sisters went down under the water, and the boy thought the whiteness he had seen was foam on the sea.

Next morning the ship sailed into port in the city of the king who ruled the foreign land.

All the church bells rang, and trumpets were blown from the tall towers, while the soldiers stood on parade with banners waving and bright bayonets fixed. There were parties every day, balls and merrymaking all the time, but the princess had not arrived yet. It was said that she was being brought up far away in a sacred temple, where she was learning every royal virtue. And at last she came home.

The little mermaid was anxious to see her beauty, and she had to admit that she had never seen anyone lovelier. The princess's skin was fine and delicate, and a pair of steadfast, blue-black eyes smiled behind her long, dark eyelashes.

"It is you!" said the prince. "You rescued me when I lay on the sea shore, left for dead!" And he clasped his blushing bride to his breast. "Oh, how happy I am!" he told the little mermaid. "The best thing in the world, the thing I never dared hope for, has come true. You will be glad of my happiness, for you wish me better than anyone else!" And the little mermaid kissed his hand and felt as if her heart would break, for his wedding morning would bring her death and turn her into foam on the sea.

All the church bells rang; heralds rode around the streets and proclaimed the wedding. Fragrant oil burned in costly silver lamps on all the altars. The priests swung censers of incense, and bride and bridegroom took each other's hands and received the bishop's blessing. The little mermaid was dressed in silk and gold and carried the bride's train, but her ears did not hear the festive music, her eyes did not see the sacred ceremony, she thought of the night of her death and all she had lost in this world.

That same evening the bride and bridegroom went on board the ship. The cannon thundered, all the flags waved, and a wonderful tent of crimson and gold with the most beautiful cushions was set up in the middle of the deck, where the bridal couple would sleep in the still, calm night.

The sails swelled in the wind, and the ship glided slowly over the clear sea. When it grew dark bright lamps were lit, and the sailors danced merry dances on deck. The little mermaid could not help remembering the first time she ever came up out of the sea and saw the same magnificence and rejoicing; and she whirled in the dance with the others, hovering like a swallow when it is pursued; and everyone applauded in admiration, for she had never before danced so beautifully. Sharp knives seemed to cut her tender feet, but she did not feel it; the pain in her heart was sharper still. She knew this was the last evening she would see the prince for whom she had left her family and her home, for whom she had sacrificed her sweet voice and suffered never-ending torment daily, although he had no idea of it. This was the last night she would breathe the same air as he did, or would set eyes on the deep sea and the sky bright with stars. An eternal night without thoughts or dreams awaited her, for she had no soul and could not win one. And all was joy and merriment on the ship until long past midnight; she laughed and danced with thoughts of death in her heart. The prince kissed his lovely bride, she toyed with his black hair, and arm in arm they went to rest in the magnificent tent.

All was still and quiet on the ship, only the steersman stood by the wheel. The little mermaid leaned her white arms on the rail and looked east towards the dawn; she knew that the first ray of the sun would kill her. Then she saw her sisters come up out of the sea; they were as pale as she was and their beautiful long hair no longer flew in the wind, for it was all cut off.

"We gave it to the witch to persuade her to help you and save you from dying tonight!" they called. "She gave us a knife – here it is! Do you see how sharp it is? Before the sun rises you must drive it into the prince's heart, and when his warm blood splashes on your feet they will grow back into a fishtail and you will be a mermaid again. Then you can come down to us in the water and live your three hundred years before you turn to salt foam on the sea. Hurry! Either he or you must die before the sun rises!

"Our old grandmother is so sad that her white hair has fallen out, just as ours fell to the witch's scissors. Kill the prince and come back! Make haste! Do you see that red streak in the sky? In a few minutes the sun will rise, and then you must die!" And they heaved a deep, strange sigh and sank into the waves.

The little mermaid pulled back the crimson fabric of the tent and saw the beautiful bride resting with her head on the prince's breast, and she bent down, kissed his fair brow, looked up at the sky where day was dawning brighter and brighter, looked at the sharp knife and then once more at the prince, who was murmuring his bride's name in his sleep. She alone was in his thoughts, and the knife shook in the mermaid's hand. But then she threw it far out to sea. The waves shone red where it fell, like drops of blood welling up from the water. Once again, as her sight failed, she looked at the prince, then she flung herself from the ship into the sea, and felt her body dissolve into foam.
Now the sun rose above the waves, its rays mild and warm on the deathly cold foam of the sea, and the little mermaid did not feel as if she were dying. She saw the bright sun, and hundreds of beautiful, translucent creatures hovering in the air above her. She could see the ship's white sails through these beings, and the red clouds in the sky; their voices were melodious but seemed to be of another world, so that no human ear could hear them and no earthly eye could see them. Their own lightness bore them up through the air without wings. The little mermaid saw that she too had a body like theirs, and she was rising up and up from the foam.

"Where am I going?" she asked, and her voice sounded like that of the beautiful beings, so other-worldly that no earthly music could suggest its sound.

"To join the daughters of the air!" they replied. "A mermaid has no immortal soul and can never get one unless she wins the love of a human being; her eternal life depends on others. The daughters of the air have no immortal souls either, but they can win a soul by doing good deeds. We are flying to the hot countries where the sultry plague-ridden air kills people, to fan them with cool breezes. We will spread the fragrance of flowers through the air and bring refreshment and healing. When we have tried to do all the good we can for three hundred years we will be granted immortal souls and share the eternal bliss of human beings. You have tried with all your heart to do good too, poor little mermaid. You have suffered and endured, you have raised yourself to the world of airy spirits, and now you can win an immortal soul after three hundred years of doing good deeds."

Then the little mermaid raised her bright arms to God's sun, and for the first time she felt tears. There were sounds on the ship again, and people stirring; she saw the prince and his beautiful bride looking for her. They gazed sadly down at the foam of the sea as if they knew she had thrown herself into the waves. Unseen, she kissed the bride's forehead, smiled at the prince, and with the other children of the air she rose up to the rose-red cloud sailing through the sky.

"In three hundred years' time we shall fly like this into the kingdom of God!" she said.

"And we may reach it even sooner!" whispered one of the daughters of the air. "We fly unseen into houses where there are children, and every time we find a good child who bring his parents joy and earns their love, God will shorten our time of trial. The child doesn't know we are flying through the house, but when we smile for joy a year is subtracted from our three hundred. But if we see a naughty, bad child then we must weep tears of grief, and every tear adds a day to the time we must serve."

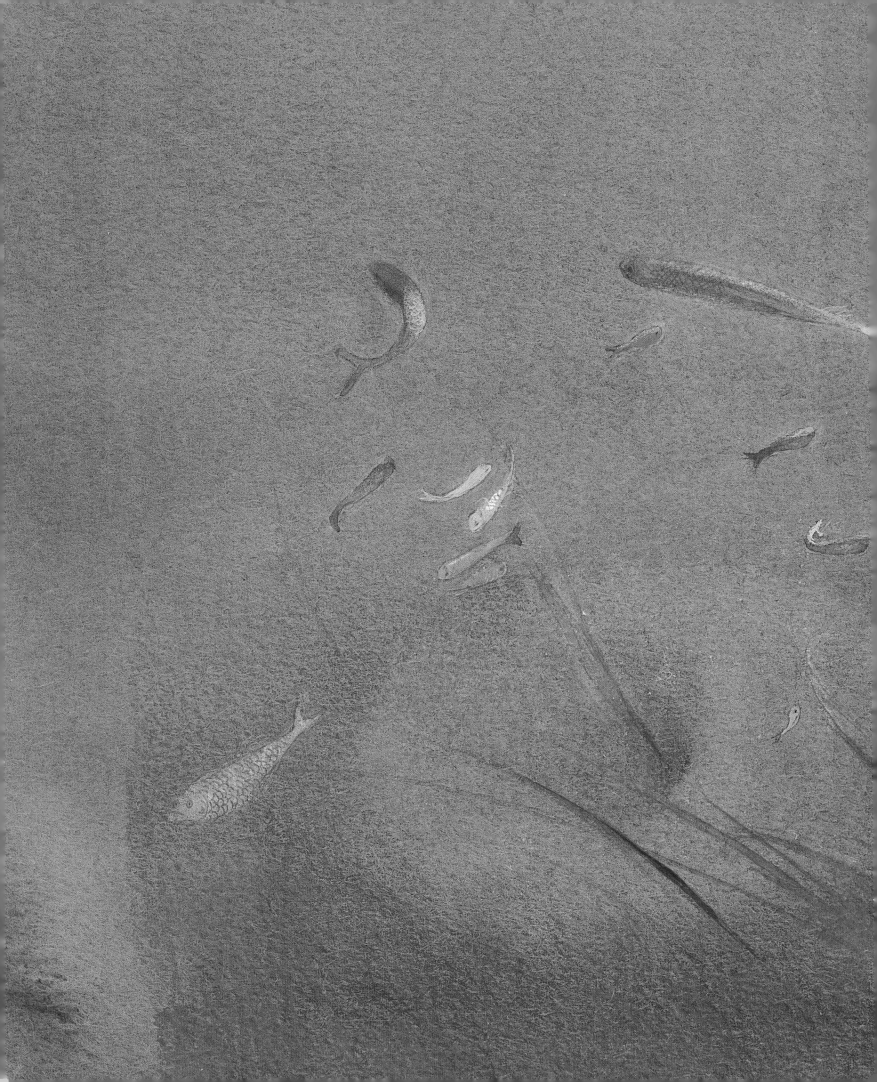